RODEO STA

Written by Sasha Quinton

Illustrated by Kenneth Callicutt

Silver Dolphin

"Well, Casey Girl. Looks like we're gonna need a new roof…"

Casey Morgan looked up at the tree limb jutting from her family's barn, and she knew her dad was right. The storm had done a lot of damage to the Morgan Ranch. It had ripped up the corral fence, felled three big trees, and even caused a small fire in one of the outbuildings. But the roof was the worst.

"We can patch it!" Casey said with more determination than hope.

"'Fraid not," her father said, "Looks like it snapped the rafter. And that's a pretty big hole." Mr. Morgan's broad shoulders seemed to sink as he spoke.

But then, he looked at Casey and smiled broadly. "No worries, kiddo," he said. "It's nothing we Morgans can't handle!" But Casey didn't believe him. Her father's smile was just a little too wide.

Casey knew her family's horse ranch had already had a tough year. With the drought in the spring and rising grain prices, they'd struggled to feed their stock. How could they afford a new roof now?

And later that night, Casey knew for sure. She heard her parents talking in the neighboring room. "Mortgage…the bank…collections…$15,000." She could only hear fragments, but it was enough. The Morgan family ranch was in trouble.

At breakfast the next morning, Casey's father pushed his eggs around his plate. Finally, he looked up and smiled at her with that same over-broad grin. "We're going to have to sell the stock," he said.

Casey dropped her fork to the floor. "Not Star!" she pleaded, before she could stop herself.

"Especially Star," her father said firmly. "Now buck up, and show some of that red-headed spirit I love."

HORSES 4 SALE

But Casey couldn't buck up. She ran from the kitchen and straight out to the back pasture. She kicked the fence post hard with her boot. "How's that for spirit?" Casey growled. But then she saw Star in the distance, and her temper melted away.

Star was the ranch's prize filly. She was the perfect American quarter horse. She stood 15 hands tall, with long sturdy legs, and strong shoulders and haunches. She had a beautiful chiseled head with a white star blazed on her forehead. And her sorrel coat was almost the exact shade of Casey's own braids!

When Star saw Casey, she whinnied keenly and raced to the fence. The feisty filly bucked playfully and tossed her head as she ran. Star skidded to a halt at the fence and nickered a happy hello. "Hey, pretty lady," Casey cooed, as she wrapped her arms around Star's warm neck.

"How can we sell such a fine horse?" Casey thought crossly. But even as she stroked Star's rich coat, she knew her father was right. It was the only way to help the ranch. And even if they did sell the stock, they still might not have enough money.

"I have to do something!" Casey declared. But what could she do?

Back in her bedroom, Casey broke open her piggy bank. "Twenty one dollars and fifty-two cents…" she groaned, "That won't fix the chicken coup!" What else could she do? A bake sale? A car wash? Babysitting? Nothing she could think of would raise enough money to fix the roof.

But later that week, Casey saw a sign at the County Fair Grounds. "RODEO: CA$H PRIZES." Casey could round a barrel better than anyone, and absolutely no horse was faster than Star! What if they entered the rodeo and won the grand prize?

When Casey got home from school, she ran straight to the corral, saddled up Star, and rode out to the back pasture. "It's the perfect place to practice!" she said and tethered Star to a tree. Star stamped her foot with curiosity and blew out hard.

Casey rolled three hay bales into the middle of the field, making a triangle. "57-58-59…" she counted as she stepped off sixty feet from the nearest bale. She marked the spot with an old rope. "There!" she said with satisfaction, "That will be the finish line. Now, are you ready for our first hay-bale barrel race?" Star whinnied happily and pranced in place.

Casey mounted up, and they took off toward the first bale.

For the next three weeks, Casey and Star practiced at every spare moment. At daybreak. After school. Between chores. Casey even brought out lanterns from the barn, so they could train after supper. And it was paying off!

They'd first worked the course at a walk-trot, but now Star rounded the bales at a full gallop. Casey couldn't believe her speed! They'd already broken the winning time from the National Finals. How could they lose?

Casey was so confident, she even remained calm when her father announced they'd found a buyer for the stock. "He's coming at noon on Saturday," he said, "We'll need to have Star and the others ready for him."

The rodeo was Saturday morning. "Sure thing!" Casey replied easily, smiling to herself.

That Saturday, Casey woke up before dawn and dressed in the dark. She pulled on her favorite jeans, her best bright blue button-down shirt, and buckled her finest belt. She crept like a field mouse from her bedroom to the kitchen, and fumbled through the pitch black looking for her hat. Finally, she felt its brim hanging from a rack on the wall. She slipped its strings around her neck, pulled on her cowboy boots, and snuck through the front door to saddle up Star.

By the time they arrived at the fairgrounds, Casey and Star were next in line for the barrel race. Casey could hear the roar from the stands as a young cowgirl careened around the last barrel to the finish line. Then the announcer called their number, and Star snorted eagerly. She was ready to race and win.

"Let's go get 'em!" Casey cheered, and she pulled up her hat from around her neck. But to her horror, it toppled to the side. Casey yanked it off and gasped. She had grabbed her father's Stetson by mistake.

What could she do? Casey glared at the hat, then set it back squarely on her head. She tightened the stampede strings, and rode boldly into the arena at top speed.

Star took off toward the first barrel at a dead run. As they neared the turn, Casey sat deep in the saddle and grabbed the horn with her left hand. She reined Star to the right. The nimble quarter horse whipped around the barrel in a perfect half circle.

But when Star bolted toward the second barrel, Casey's hat lurched forward. It tottered on her forehead, then fell right in her face. Casey couldn't see a thing!

The crowd gasped in unison. But there was nothing Casey could do. For just a second, she thought to rein Star in and forfeit. But her red-headed spirit kicked in. She wouldn't let blind luck stop them! She tightened her grip on the horn, gave Star her head, and squeezed hard with her legs. "Hee-ya!" she cried, "Go, Star, go!"

Star charged forward and whipped left around the second barrel. Then, she sprinted through the middle to the back of the arena. Casey hugged Star's ribs tightly with her legs, trying to keep her seat. Star tore around the last drum in a perfect clover-leaf pattern. Then, she thundered through the center, heading for home.

As they crossed the finish line, the crowd exploded. Star skidded to a stop, and Casey finally tipped back her father's hat. She saw the audience on their feet, leaping and shouting wildly. "At 13.52 seconds, we have a winner," the loudspeaker boomed. Casey swung down from the saddle and threw her arms around Star's neck.

The head judge ran toward them. "That was quite a ride, little lady," he puffed, out of breath.

"It was all Star, sir," Casey declared, "She's the star of the rodeo!"

"Well, then," the judge replied happily, "This is a fitting prize." And he handed Casey a shiny, silver belt-buckle shaped like a star. Casey slipped the buckle through Star's breast collar and kissed her downy nose.

"And to think," the judge said with a chuckle, "All this before noon!"

Noon?!? Casey looked down at her watch in panic. It was 11:53. She had to get back to the ranch!

She leapt back in the saddle, and whipped Star around, ready to go. "Wait!" cried the judge, holding up a check, "You forgot your prize money!" Casey snatched it from his hands, without even looking, and raced down the road.

By the time Casey and Star reached the Morgan family ranch, the buyer was already there—stock loaded and ready to go. He stood on the front lawn with Mr. and Mrs. Morgan. His cheeks were red and arms waving wildly. Casey knew he was looking for Star.

Star slid to a stop, and Casey swung down into the gravel. She ran across the lawn as fast as her tired feet would carry her, launching into her father's arms.

"Dad...the roof...a check...we won...." Casey could barely form a sentence, but she held up the crumpled check beneath his nose.

Mr. Morgan pried the check from her fingers, and opened it quickly. "$2,500!" he read with surprise. He looked from Casey in her show clothes, to Star, to the silver buckle on her breastplate, and seemed to understand.

But Casey's heart sank. Star was worth ten times more than that. And $2,500 was nowhere near enough to fix the roof.

"I take it this is my filly?" the buyer interrupted, impatient to go. Mr. Morgan looked at him and grinned.

"I'm sorry, sir," he said, never taking his eyes off Casey, "But this horse isn't for sale. She's a rodeo star! Besides, I can't separate my redheads." The buyer turned on his heels, climbed into his truck, and slammed the door. He drove off quickly, leaving Casey, her parents, and Star in a cloud of gravel dust.

"But Dad," Casey coughed, "My check isn't enough to fix the roof! How will we manage?"

"Well, kiddo," he replied, "It's nothing we Morgans can't handle!" And this time, his smile was big, broad, and warm.

Casey believed him.

All About Barrel Racing

★ Barrel racing is a rodeo event in which horse and rider try
to complete a clover-leaf pattern around three barrels.

★ In barrel racing, the fastest time wins.

★ Times are measured by either an "electronic eye,"
a laser device, or by a judge who drops a flag.

★ The timer begins when horse and rider cross
the start line.

★ The timer stops when the horse and rider complete the
clover-leaf and cross the finish line.

★ The barrels are placed in a triangle in the center
of the arena.

★ If a horse or rider hits or knocks over a barrel, a time
penalty of five seconds is applied.

★ Barrel racing originally developed as an event for
women and girls.

What to Wear in a Rodeo

★ Long-sleeved shirt (sleeves rolled down, buttoned or snapped, and shirt tails tucked in)
★ Western hat
★ Cowboy boots
★ Western denim pants or Western dress pants

Optional:

★ Spurs
★ Necktie
★ Chaps
★ Safety helmet

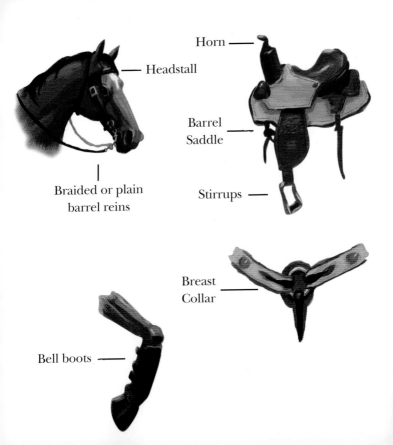

Horn

Headstall

Barrel
Saddle

Stirrups

Braided or plain
barrel reins

Breast
Collar

Bell boots

Meet the American Quarter Horse

★ The American quarter horse is famous for sprinting short distances.

★ Quarter horses got their name by outrunning other breeds in quarter mile races.

★ They excel as show horses, racehorses, rodeo competitors, work horses, and family horses.

★ The quarter horse stands between 14 and 16 hands tall.

★ Most quarter horses are strong, stocky, compact, broad chested, and well-muscled.

★ Quarter horses have a very sensible, intelligent temperament.